Sh...
wit...

by Geo...
illustrated by L... ...e

Sam's house

the supermarket

2

to the
school

to Emily's house

to the
museum

to Lin's
apartment

Con's house

3

Hi, my name is Con.

This is my family.

Chapter 1
Shopping with Dad!

Saturday is the day we go to the supermarket. Most of the time Mum does the shopping, but today Dad is doing the shopping.

My sister Maria says, '*Dad* is doing the shopping!'
My brother Tom says, '*Dad* is doing the shopping!'
I say, '*Dad* is doing the shopping! Can I come too?'

'Yes, Con,' says Dad. 'I'll show you
how it is done.'
Mum says, 'You'll be sorry.' I don't
know if she is talking to me or Dad.

Chapter 2
Door Trouble

When we get to the supermarket
I go to get the shopping trolley.
Dad says, 'I will go inside.'

I think I can get inside the shop, Con.

I tell Dad that supermarket doors
can be tricky. I say that supermarket
doors can do their own thing. I say
maybe you should wait for me, just to
be on the safe side. Dad says, 'I think
I can get inside the shop, Con.'

Dad goes in through the out door.
The out door shuts on Dad.
Dad is stuck in the out door. I say,
'Don't worry, Dad. I will get
someone to save you.'

Ms Green, who works in the
supermarket, helps Dad get
out of the door.
'Thanks, Ms Green,' I say. I tell
Dad to thank Ms Green too.
'Thanks,' says Dad.

Dad says there should be signs
about the dangerous doors.

Chapter 3
Too many Beans

I push the trolley. Dad says, 'Let me push the trolley Con.'
I tell Dad that these trolleys are tricky.
I say that these trolleys want to do their own thing. I say maybe I should push the trolley, just to be on the safe side.

Dad says, 'I think I can push a trolley, Con.'

I give the trolley to Dad.
Dad crashes the trolley. He crashes into
a hundred cans of beans. A hundred
cans of beans crash to the floor.
A hundred cans of beans crash
onto Dad.

I say, 'Don't worry, Dad. I will get
someone to save you.'

Ms Green helps Dad get out
from under the cans.
'Thanks, Ms Green,' I say. I tell
Dad to thank Ms Green too.
'Thanks,' says Dad.

Dad says they should put new
wheels on the trolleys.

Chapter 4
Orange Crush

'We need some fruit,' says Dad. I push the trolley to the fruit stand.
'Stop, Con,' says Dad. 'We need to buy some oranges.'

I tell Dad that oranges can be tricky. I say that oranges can do their own thing. I say maybe I should put the oranges into the bag, just to be on the safe side. Dad says, 'I think I can put oranges into a bag, Con.'

Dad picks an orange from the bottom of the stack. Hundreds of oranges roll all over the floor. Hundreds of oranges roll all over Dad.

I say, 'Don't worry, Dad. I will get someone to save you.'

Ms Green helps Dad get out from
under the oranges.
'Thanks, Ms Green,' I say. I tell
Dad to thank Ms Green too.
'Thanks,' says Dad.

Dad says they need to stack
the oranges better.

Chapter 5

Deep Freeze

Next we look for the ice-cream. I push the trolley to the freezer. Dad looks into the freezer.

I think I can get ice-cream out of the freezer, Con.

I say getting ice-cream from the freezer can be tricky. I say that freezers can do their own thing. I say maybe I should get the ice-cream out of the freezer, just to be on the safe side. Dad says, 'I think I can get ice-cream out of the freezer, Con.'

Dad leans into the freezer. Dad
falls into the freezer. Dad is stuck
in the freezer.

I say, 'Don't worry, Dad. I will get
someone to save you.'

Ms Green helps Dad get out of
the freezer.
'Thanks, Ms Green,' I say. I tell
Dad to thank Ms Green too.
'Thanks,' says Dad.

Dad says they should not have
freezers at the supermarket.

At the checkout I say,
'Goodbye, Ms Green.'
I tell Dad to say goodbye to
Ms Green too.

'Goodbye,' says Dad.
'See you next time,' says Ms Green,
'with your mother ... PLEASE!'

20

'Thanks for taking me shopping,'
I say to Dad. 'You really showed
me how it's done!'

Survival Tips

Tips for surviving the supermarket

1 Read the signs on the door. Go in the in door and not in the out door.

2 Choose a trolley that has the wheels all going the same way.

3 Stay away from the cans of beans.

4 Stay away from the oranges.

5 Stay away from the freezer.

6 Don't leave your trolley in the middle of the aisle. You might cause a traffic jam.

7 If you have a dad like Con's, don't take him shopping.

Riddles and Jokes

Sam Why don't bananas get lonely?
Con Because they hang around in bunches.

Con What did one orange sitting in the sun say to the other orange sitting in the sun?
Sam I am starting to peel.

Sam What lives in the freezer and squeaks?
Con Mice-icles!

Con Why can't you tell secrets in the supermarket?
Sam Because corn has ears, potatoes have eyes and beanstalk.